DAYAL KAUR KHALSA

GREEN CAT

Tundra Books

Copyright © 2002 by the Estate of Dayal Kaur Khalsa

Published in Canada by Tundra Books,
481 University Avenue, Toronto, Ontario M5G 2E9

Published in the United States by Tundra Books of Northern New York,
P.O. Box 1030, Plattsburgh, New York 12901

Library of Congress Control Number: 2001095374

National Library of Canada Cataloguing in Publication Data

Khalsa, Dayal Kaur, 1943-1989
   Green cat

ISBN 0-88776-586-6

   I. Title.

PS8571.H36G74 2002   jC813'.54   C2001-903542-X
PZ7.K52647Gr 2002

We acknowledge the support of the Canada Council for the Arts and the Ontario Arts Council for our publishing program.

We acknowledge the financial support of the Government of Canada through the Book Publishing Industry Development Program for our publishing activities.

Design: Terri Nimmo

Printed in Hong Kong, China

1 2 3 4 5 6   07 06 05 04 03 02

Tom and Lynn shared a room.   "I want more space!" each one would shout,
They thought it was too small.   And try to toss the other out, into the drafty hall.

One night as they got set to fight,

A tall green cat stopped by.

He asked, "What do you like the most?"

Tom and Lynn responded, "Toast!"

He said, "Well, so do I."

Green Cat went and got the toaster,
The kitchen table, chairs, a poster.

He said, "The best is yet to come,"
And brought two packages of gum.

Napkins, plates, a spoon and honey,   A bale of hay and a pig
A floor lamp, wall map, and – what's funny –   (though it wasn't very big).

Four flapping flags, nine napping cats,
Six silly geese in party hats.

A little Leaning Tower of Pisa,
A potted palm, the Mona Lisa.

A bunch of bananas, a bowl of spaghetti,
Two dotted dalmatians, a burst of confetti.

A rowboat, a rainbow,
A little red calf,

Then, just for a laugh,
He brought a giraffe.

From a corner of the clutter,
Tom and Lynn were heard to mutter,

In voices muffled dim as doom,
"We . . . need . . . more . . . room!"

Out went the tower, bananas, confetti,
Dalmatians, the picture, the palm, the spaghetti,

The geese and the rowboat, the flags and the cats,
The pig and the hay and the rainbow and hats,

The floor lamp, the wall map, the spoon and the toaster,
The plates and the napkins, the table, the poster,

The chairs and the honey, the bread, gum, and calf,

And finally Green Cat
took away the giraffe.

"Enough room now?" Green Cat asked.
"Yes, yes!" said Tom and Lynn.
He hugged them both with all his might,
Turned off the light
And said, "Good night,
Until we meet again."

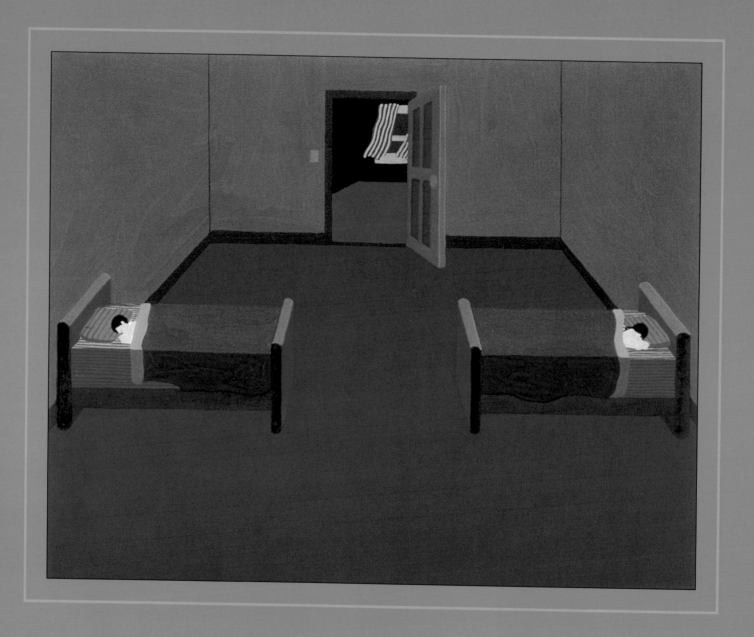

They lay upon their little beds, but sleep did not come soon.
They tossed and turned for half the night.

Said Tom, "The room does not feel right."
Said Lynn, "There's too much room."

And so they tiptoed down the stairs,

And brought back up the kitchen chairs.